THE DENNIS THE MENACE BOOK 1996

Printed and Published in Great Britain by D. C. Thomson & Co. Ltd., 185 Fleet Street, London EC4A 2HS. © D. C. Thomson & Co. Ltd., 1995

ISBN 0-85116-604 0

MEALS ON WHEELS

YOU'VE READ THE BOOK, EATEN THE THE T-SHIRT, SWITCHED ON THE LAMP AND ...THE MENACE MERCHANDISE YOU *CAN'T* BUY!

TRICKY TREATS

What's on MTV

(Menace Television)

7.00
THE PIG BREAKFAST
Live coverage of Rasher scoffing yesterday's curry, custard, potato peelings and congealed gravy.
WARNING:— Not for viewers of a nervous disposition.

9.00
KILLJOY
Dad and an invited studio audience moan at Dennis for half an hour telling him not to break anything, not to make a mess, not to frighten Softies, not to skip off school . . . not to have fun in other words.

9.30
NEWS AND SPORT
Dad's chance to catch up on current events is ruined when Dennis's football goes a bit off line.

10.00
FROST IN THE MORNING
David Frost puts it to Dennis the Menace that his anti-social predilections countermine authoritarianism. Dennis counters his argument by splatting him with an over-ripe tomato in the kisser.

12.00
THE TRAVEL SHOW
Walter the Softy discovers the delights of Timbuctoo when he's sent there by parcel post by Dennis.

1.00
FILM: NEEPLESS IN SEATTLE
A Scottish pig (movingly played by Rasher) is distraught when he visits a city on the west coast of America only to find they are fresh out of turnips.

5.00
BLACK AND BLUE PETER
Peter Sissons comes off worst when he disagrees with Dennis's Gran in a debate about the price of mint humbugs.

6.00
THE DRIPPED ON FACTOR
Walter and chummies perform various intellectual tasks while Dennis tries to soak them with his water pistol.

6.45
POT BLACK
Gnipper gets stuck in Mum's stew pan while trying to pinch Dad's supper.

7.30
POP AT THE TOPS
Dennis fires corks from his pop gun at several soppy music stars as they try to perform their latest releases.

8.00
GRIMEWATCH
Sue Cook and Nick Ross are at the ringside as Dennis and his mate Curly have a full scale mud fight.

8.30
GRIMEWASH
Mum and Dad give the mud covered contestants a bath and get a big surprise — it's not Dennis and his pal under all that mud . . . it's Sue Cook and Nick Ross.

9.00
WHEELS OF MISFORTUNE
Nicky Campbell gets a shock to find the wheels of the luxury limo star prize have gone missing.

9.30
DENNIS THE MENACE'S INDYCARTIE '96
Dennis tries out some new tyres he's just 'acquired'.

10.00
CHEERS . . .
. . . from Mum and Dad cos Dennis has gone to bed at last!

SHOOTING-STARS

POLITE PORKER

At home—

HIS FAVOURITE—MOULDY CABBAGE AND PRUNES!

RASHER'S TROUGH

But—

HOW DISGUSTING!

THIS IS MORE LIKE IT!

CRAB PATÉ

MY EXPENSIVE LUNCH!

DELICATE GUZZLE!

Then—

MUST GO AND FRESHEN UP.

BATHROOM

BATHROOM

EAU DE NIFF

SCENT FROM PARIS

TALC

YAWN! TIME FOR A WELL-MANNERED, AFTER-DINNER NAP.

THIS LOOKS NICE AND COMFY.

GASP! YOU'RE PUTTING ON WEIGHT, MUM!

SNORE! GRUNTLE!

THAT DOES IT! I WANT HIM THE WAY HE WAS!

GASP!

FOR A SLIGHT INCREASE IN POCKET MONEY, THAT COULD BE ARRANGED.

So—

THIS IS A COMPOST HEAP— PIGS ROLL ABOUT IN IT...

COMPOST HEAP

DENNIS'S SCHOOL OF BAD MANNERS

INSIDE JOB

HUH! I'M FED UP BEING KEPT IN FOR BEING BOTTOM OF THE CLASS— WISH I WAS OUT IN THE SUN.

SOFTIES

SKIP

PRANCE

Next day—

NERVOUS REX

Suddenly—

BOO!

GNOO!

GNASHEE!

HAR-HAR!

OO! WH-WHAT A F-FRIGHT!

WAIT FOR IT!

WALTER— SOFTEST OF THEM ALL

SKIP

DAISY

I KNEW HE'D TRIP OVER THAT DAISY!

TRIP

WE'LL BORROW THESE FOR A WHILE!

SOB! I CAN'T FIND MY GLASSES!

In class—

OH, DEAR! I'VE LOST MY PEN!

SPOTTY PERKINS

GNEE-HEE!

HERE—BORROW MY SPARE ONE.

HOW KIND!

NOW FOR THE CLASS EXAM.

TEACHER WILL NEVER BE ABLE TO READ THAT SHAKY WRITING!

STILL FRIGHTENED

TREMBLE

SHAKE

WALTER CAN'T SEE WHERE TO WRITE!

WALTER'S PAPER →

THAT PEN I GAVE SPOTTY MAKES BIG BLOTS!

I WON'T BE BOTTOM IN THIS EXAM!

DISGRACEFUL WORK— AS BAD AS DENNIS'S!

YOU'LL ALL STAY IN AFTER SCHOOL!

AW!

HUH! I'M STILL NOT OUTSIDE IN THE SUN...

... AND NOW I'M INSIDE IN THE "RAIN"!

WAIL!

BOO-HOO!

SOB!

SEE YOU LATER.

YAH!

CHEEK!

SQUEAK!

GNASH!

MY HAIR! LOOK WHAT YOU'VE DONE, GNASHER!

Meanwhile—

WHAT A LAUGH!

S-SEE-Y-YOU AT THE MATHS EXAM TOMORROW.

MATHS EXAM?

FULL HORROR

CAN'T LET OUR FRIENDS SEE US LIKE THIS!

So— HURRY UP—YOU'VE GOT TO GUM MY HAIR BACK NEXT!

THAT'S TWO PINK LOLLIPOPS YOU OWE ME AS PAYMENT!

PLEASANT PRESENTS

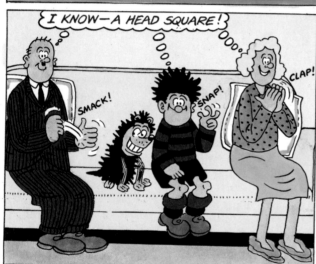

LOVE thy NEIGHBOUR

IT'S A BEAUTIFUL HOUSE — CENTRALLY HEATED DOOR KNOBS, DOUBLE-GLAZED FISH TANK, FULLY CARPETED COAL SHED..

THE HOUSE OWNER

HOUSE FOR SALE

..AND JUST LOOK AT THE LOVELY GARDEN.

SEEN OUR BALL?

AARGH! IT'S NEXT DOOR TO HIM!

GROAN!

WHO WILL BUY THIS HOUSE WITH THOSE MENACES AS NEIGHBOURS?

HOUSE FOR SALE

TRAMPLE

I'M JUST BACK FROM TEN YEARS IN DARKEST AFRICA—MUST BUY A HOUSE.

STANLEY LIVINGSTON — EXPLORER

AH, NICE PLACE!

HOUSE FOR SALE

LET'S JUST HOPE HE DOESN'T SEE DENNIS AND GNASHER!

HI! WE LIVE NEXT DOOR!

HOUSE FOR SALE

OH, NO!

GASP! I DON'T BELIEVE IT!
I'M GOING MOUNTAINEERING.
WALTER, SOFTEST OF SOFTIES

HAR-HAR! A MOLE-HILL'S A MOUNTAIN TO A SOFTY!

PHEW! MADE IT!
SILENT MIRTH
PROD

HOI! WHO BONKED ME?
HAR! HAR!
EEK!

I FANCY MOUNTAINEERING—TROUBLE IS, BEANOTOWN IS AS FLAT AS A PANCAKE.
GNESH!

I KNOW—I'LL BUILD MY OWN MOUNTAIN! DAD'S COMPOST HEAP WILL DO FOR A START.

GIVE US A GOAL, DUFFERS UNITED!

THERE'S NOT MANY PEOPLE HERE TO WATCH. READ ON AND FIND OUT WHY — *THEY'RE RUBBISH!*

The Midfield

AND THIS GAME LOOKS LIKE GETTING BOGGED DOWN IN MIDFIELD!

YIPPEE! WE LOVE A NICE BOG!

Rasher and Smudge

MATCH ABANDONED!

SPLUDGE!

SPLASH IT ALL OVER!

The Defenders

NICE DEFENSIVE WALL. BUT IT NEEDS SOMETHING!

LIKE SOME NICE DECORATIVE SUN FLOWERS, SWEET PEAS AND PANSYS.

LOVELY, WALTER!

WELL, I THINK SO!

MUMMY!

BLAM!

EEK!

KEEPING MUM

MUM HAS FLU. YOU'LL HAVE TO HELP AROUND THE HOUSE WHILE I'M AT WORK.

HMPH!

AATISHOOO!

HOME SWEET HOME

BEANO

WANT A GAME OF FAMILIES, WALTER? I'LL LET YOU BE MUM.

GOODY!

SOFT LITTLE FELLOW

SO— WASH MY FOOTBALL STRIP, MUM!

EH?

TRA-LA-LA!

BEANO

SCRUB

SOON— GLERK! IT'S SHRUNK! DIDN'T YOU READ THE WASHING INSTRUCTIONS?

SILLY ME!

STILL, IT FITS MY TEDDY NICELY!

GLURK!

Wet! Wet! Wet!

DENNIS'S SCHOOL TRIP

Dennis's teacher was not a happy man. Things were bad enough for him on a normal school day — in fact they were terrible on a normal school day — particularly if Dennis turned up on time and the teacher had to put up with him till four o'clock. What was even worse, though, was the annual class outing.

The year they had gone to a safarai park Dennis had scared the animals so much by pulling faces at them, that they had all tried to hide up a tree. As the park had at least a dozen elephants this had caused a few trees to fall down.

The year they had gone to a dolphinarium, Dennis had taught one of the dolphins to try to leap through the large hoop earrings one of the other teachers was wearing, rather than the hoop its trainer was holding out. It didn't quite get through the earring but it did manage to knock her wig off.

This year the teacher had had an idea. He had found an organisation called 'Tough Tours' to take Dennis on a separate trip from the rest of the class. They specialised in courses in wrestling with lions, surfing over waterfalls and other really stupid things. Even at this place the staff weren't totally stupid, though. Most of them read the Beano and knew all about Dennis, so were having nothing to do with him.

Only one guide did not know about him. This was because he was so tough he had to be brought up by tigers and could only read tiger language. Since tigers never read the Beano, as they are cats and don't like Gnasher, he had never heard of Dennis. This was why he agreed to take Dennis on a trip.

He was the man who took the climbing trips, so Dennis's teacher asked him to take Dennis up Mount Everest in the hope that they would get lost and never come back.

Dennis was delighted and packed Gnasher and Gnipper in his rucksack before getting on the plane. The guide was so tough and strong that he did not notice that Dennis had packed Rasher in his rucksack.

Normally going up Everest involves a long walk to get to the bottom of the mountain. Dennis cleverly avoided this by letting Gnasher, Gnipper and Rasher out on the plane. Gnasher and Gnipper thought the pilots' uniforms looked like a postie's and so gave them a gnashing while Rasher ate so many of the passengers' meals that his burps were shaking all the rivets out of the plane. All of this annoyed the stewardess so much that Dennis and company, together with the guide who was so tough that he pretended not to be bothered (there was a bit of a tear in his eye when Rasher touched down though).

The guide thought a bit of hard climbing would soon sort Dennis out. Climbing with your pets isn't difficult though. Gnasher bit out steps in the ice for Dennis. Gnipper used his sharp tooth as an ice pick so that Dennis could pull himself up the steeper bits. Rasher followed behind so that if anyone fell they would bounce off him and shoot back up again.

In no time they were up to the height where they needed oxygen. This made the guide giggle unstoppably — not because anything was funny, but because Dennis had replaced his oxygen bottle with laughing gas.

FLOAT

Dennis used his oxygen to inflate Rasher and then used him as a balloon to float himself and his pets to the summit, leaving behind the guide, who was now laughing louder than Walter on the day he had seen Dennis's school report. WARNING! (Do not try inflating a pig in this way at home. It is a technique that only really works on cartoon pigs).

It was very cold on the summit. There should have been plenty of clothes in their rucksacks but unfortunately Dennis had had to leave something behind in order to get Gnasher, Gnipper, Rasher and the kitchen sink in. (Rasher had used the kitchen sink as a trough on the plane, stupid. How else would a pig eat?)

By a slightly unusual stroke of luck they were not cold for long. As there was not much room on the summit, Dennis had to stand on top of Rasher while Gnasher and Gnipper perched on his arms. This made them look like a pretty ferocious monster to anyone who was too stupid to know what a boy and two dogs look like when they are standing on a pig. The Abominable Snowman who lives at the top of Everest had seen many things, including the Italian Motorcycle Display Team Everest Expedition of 1932 form a human pyramid and the 1974 Come Dancing Expedition do an eightsome reel.

However, he had never seen a boy and two dogs standing on a pig, so naturally he thought the worst and screamed loudly before jumping out of his skin. Dennis and company grabbed the skin and in no time were warm.

JUMPED OUT OF SKIN

The Abominable Snowman (who wasn't really made out of snow — you don't really believe any of that nonsense, do you?) was pretty cold without his skin. Dennis is a great fan of anyone who is naughty enough to have Abominable as a first name and so was keen to help. Luckily the guide was so tough that he did not need the coat that Dennis grabbed from him and so was happy to give it to the Snowman. He was keeping pretty warm anyway by laughing uproariously as he still had the laughing gas on.

PLONK

SNATCH!

In fact the more the guide thought about the prospect of spending any more time with Dennis the more he gave to the Snowman. Soon he had given him the air tickets home, all the climbing gear and the keys to his house in Beanotown. All he kept was the laughing gas — not that he really needed it any more — the sight of the Snowman in his clothes, which were very unfashionable and in a horrible purple floral pattern, was enough to make anyone laugh.

The guide had worked out that he was far less likely to encounter Dennis ever again if he stayed on Everest, so it was the Snowman who went back to Beanotown with Dennis. His table manners and so on would have usually raised some suspicion on the plane, but since Dennis and his pets were sitting close to him he actually managed to look quite civilised by comparison. Tough Tours were delighted. Their new climbing guide was very good at climbing and, once Dennis had given him back his fur, didn't wear the horrible purple clothes that the previous instructor had.

Dennis's teacher was pretty disappointed that Dennis had managed to get back at all. In fact, very disappointed — he cried for three days and bit the legs off his desk. He has now got over it and is trying to arrange a trip to Mars in an open topped rocket with very little fuel and a pilot with a fear of heights and no sense of direction for Dennis next year . . . Keep trying, Teacher!

Softly, Softly

PANTO TIME

Saturday morning –

I'LL TAKE YOU TO THE MATINEE OR A PANTOMIME THIS AFTERNOON. THINK ABOUT WHICH ONE YOU'D LIKE TO SEE.

Soon–

POOR FLUFFY. YOUR LITTLE PAWS ARE COLD WITH ALL THIS NASTY SNOW!

WALTER·SOFT·BOY

THESE WILL KEEP THEM WARMER!

DOLLS' BOOTS

SQUEAL! GNASHER'S AFTER POOR FLUFFY!

CLUMP!

CLUMP!

THESE BOOTS GIVE YOU A SUPER GRIP!

GNERK! PAWS DON'T!

SCREECH!

SLIDE

HEH-HEH!

OOOMF!

HMM! THINK WE CAN CROSS "PUSS IN BOOTS" OFF OUR LIST OF PANTOMIMES TO VISIT.

GNASHER'S SALES

PATHETIC PETS GNEED GIBBER GNO LONGER, THANKS TO 'GNASHER TEETH' — THE GNOVELTY GNASHERS. EACH SET IS LOVINGLY GNASH-CRAFTED FROM STEEL GIRDERS. WEARERS WILL BE AMAZED AT THE TRANSFORMATION. JUST LOOK AT THE SATISFIED CUSTOMERS BELOW!

CASE STUDY 1: TIDDLES

BEFORE

AFTER

I used to watch helplessly as dogs raided our dustbin and ran off with my scraps. I desperately needed a change of image . . .

. . . 'Gnasher Teeth' gave me the confidence to reclaim my territory. Now I can stroll into the fish-mongers, with my head held high, and make off with their best salmon!

PLEASE RUSH ME A SET OF "GNASHER TEETH". I AM OVER 105 YEARS OF AGE. I ENCLOSE A CHEQUE FOR TWELVE DOG BISCUITS PAYABLE TO: **GNASHER, THE KENNEL, DENNIS'S HOUSE, BEANOTOWN.**

GNAME _____

ADDRESS _____

All applications will be treated with the strictest confidence. "GNASHER TEETH" will be sent to your home in a plain brown envelope.

<u>PLEASE TICK</u>
- ☐ I WOULD LIKE TO KNOW MORE ABOUT GNASHER PRODUCTS
- ☐ GNO GNUNK MAIL
- ☐ I UNDERSTAND THIS OFFER IS **TOTALLY** FALSE. ISN'T GNASHER A MENACE FOR RAISING OUR HOPES LIKE THIS?

CASE STUDY 2: HAROLD

BEFORE

AFTER

I was tired of barking up the wrong tree. Cats laughed and mongrels mocked. At one stage I couldn't even chase my own tail . . .

. . . then a friend suggested I try 'Gnasher Teeth'! Oh, boy! Did they make a difference! Nowadays postmen scream when my name's mentioned. In fact my owners' haven't had any mail for the past 6 months!

CASE STUDY 3: WHISKEY

BEFORE

AFTER

Sniff! Other gerbils used to kick sawdust in my face. By the time I got to the waterbottle it was full of crumbs . . .

. . . then I discovered 'Gnasher teeth'! Now no rodent messes with me, and I'm always first at the wheel!

SEND ɢNO MONEY ɢNOW!!!

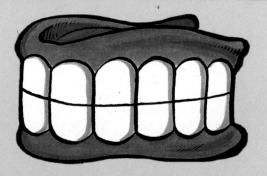

IGLOOS ARE WARM, I'M TOLD.

IGLOO

So—

IT'S COMING ON FINE.

GOLD-FISH POND

Eventually—

THERE—IN YOU GO.

PUFFSH! GASPSH!

But—

GNASHER'S SO HOT HE'S MELTED THE IGLOO!

EH?

HERE'S DAD.

WHAT'S WRONG, LAD?

CAN'T FIND ANY PLACE FOR GNASHER TO SLEEP!

WHERE IS GNASHER?

ERK! MAYBE HE'S LEFT HOME!

I SHOULD BE SO LUCKY!

HEY! WHERE'S THAT MUSIC COMING FROM?

HAR-HAR! THINK HE'S FOUND A PLACE TO SLEEP!

COSY

GASP! MUM'S PUT THE HEATING FULL UP FOR HER PRECIOUS PLANTS!

VERY WARM

HEAT

GNASP! I NEED WATER!

AND SHE USES ALL SORTS OF CONTAINERS TO GROW THEM IN!

GNASHER

I'VE HAD ENOUGH OF THESE PLANTS!

ZZZZ

I'LL PUT THIS CLIMBING PLANT HERE—

TWITCH

TWITCH

Later—

—IT'S KEEN TO GET TO WORK!

HELP! HELP! SET ME FREE!

WE'LL FREE YOU IF YOU GET RID OF THESE PLANTS.

OK! ANYTHING TO GET FREE!

GNASH!

WELL DONE, GNASHER!

RECOIL

RECOIL

RECOIL

Soon—

STANLEY LIVINGSTONE, EXPLORER, DENNIS'S NEIGHBOUR.

GLUM

GLUM

HI, STANLEY— WHAT'S THE PROBLEM?

CARRUTHERS

WE MISS THE JUNGLE, DENNIS!

NOT TO WORRY—I CAN HELP!

'BYE, SWEETHEARTS!

PLOD

THANKS, DENNIS—YOU CAN COME AND PLAY AT TARZAN ANY TIME YOU WANT!

AND I CAN SEE MY PRECIOUS PLANTS WHEN I WANT TO!

ANYTHING TO HELP

Early one morning—

ZZNN

Z!

GNZ!
GNZ!
GNZ!
GNZ!

HAVING A MENACE AS A SON CAN HAVE ITS USES.

SANDPAPER

YAHOO! SATURDAY MORNING!

TRING

GNASHOO!

NICELY SANDED DOWN— JUST AS I PLANNED!

Then—

WHAT?

CHEEK!

THAT'S THE CAR CLEANED!

SOCCER SHOCKER

EEAGH! MY MASTERPIECE!

PEA-FLAVOURED ICE-CREAM! YEUCH!

PLOP! PLOP!

PEAS

MIGHT AS WELL HAVE SOME TARGET PRACTICE ON THE WAY TO THE MATCH.

DENNIS'S FOOTBALL KIT

PONK!

At the game—

BOOT!

CATCH IT, PIE-FACE!

WHY DIDN'T YOU CATCH IT?

THE ELASTIC IN MY SHORTS HAS BURST!

GULP! I'M SORRY, DENNIS.

HMM!

THAT'LL HOLD YOUR SHORTS UP.

Soon—

PEA

SPLURT!

YUM! I'M FOND OF PEAS!

CAN'T CONTINUE THE GAME WITHOUT THE PEA FOR MY WHISTLE!

THIS SHOULD FIX IT!

PEAS

GREAT! NOW WHERE WAS I?..

PEAS

PEEP!

...AH, YES! DENNIS COMMITTED A FOUL!

HUH!

PEAS

After the game—

SORRY, BOYS—THE SHOWERS AREN'T WORKING.

CHANGING ROOMS AND SHOWERS

But—

YAHOO!

SUPER SHOWER!

HOT WATER

DENNIS, I'VE HAD COMPLAINTS ABOUT YOU AND YOUR WEAPONS!

HAND THEM OVER!

NO, NO! DON'T TAKE THEM! PLEASE! PLEASE!

GASP!

WE ALL AGREE!

SHOWERS

OUT OF HIS TREE

I'LL LOB IT OVER GNASHER'S HEAD.

JAMMED

AW! OUR BALL'S STUCK!

HEY, REX—COME HERE A MINUTE!

NERVOUS REX—SOFTY

OO! D-DON'T SHOUT—IT FRIGHTENS ME!

WH-WHAT IS IT?

PIN

SQUEAL!

TINY NOISE!

WHILE YOU'RE UP THERE—THROW OUR BALL DOWN!

HEH-HEH! CLEVER, EH?

PUSH

BED SPREAD

WALTER'S GONE ENVIRONMENTAL!

SWINISH STENCH!

PERFUMED PANSY SEEDS.

SCATTER!

MUCKY PIGS ARE SUCH AN EYESORE AND A NOSESORE!

A QUICK PERM CAN MAKE THE WORLD OF DIFFERENCE!

LITTLE HAIR-DRESSER

AN OLD RUSTY PRAM CAN BE TRANSFORMED . . .

TOWN DUMP

PERFUME PONG!

THEY'RE WONDERFUL FOR SCATTERING PETALS!

ROSE PETALS.

WHIRR!

OLD POLYTHENE BA[G]
SHOULD NEVER B[E]
THROWN AWAY . .

WARMTH!

SPROUT!

A FEW SEEDS AND A HEAT LAMP MAKE THEM LOOK OH, SO PRETTY!

OVERGROWN PLANTS CAN BE UNSIGHTLY!

... INTO A LOVELY SAILING BOAT FOR YOUR SOFT TOYS!

S.S. SOFTY

BOB! FLOAT!

OLD BIKES NEEDN'T BE TOSSED OUT.

... THEY MAKE SUCH LOVELY BALLET LEOTARDS. EXTREMELY HANDY FOR ESCAPING DENNIS'S CLUTCHES!

LEAP!

PRANCE!

SKIP!

GRACEFUL CAVORTINGS!

NEW KID ON THE BLOCK

I'M NEW IN BEANOTOWN. WONDER IF I CAN MAKE ANY FRIENDS?

A NEW CHAPPIE. WONDER IF HE'S A NICE BOY LIKE US?

WONDER IF THIS NEW FELLOW'S TOUGH LIKE US?

SOFTIES

MENACES →

So— ARE YOU A MENACE?...

...OR A SOFTY?

ER—I'M NOT SURE!

LET'S SEE IF YOU LIKE KNITTING.

THIS IS FUN!

GROAN!

HE'S A SOFTY!

CLICK! CLICK!

GNUMPH!

LOOK WHAT I'VE KNITTED!

OOOH! A NASTY HORRIBLE SPIDER!

HEH-HEH! MAYBE HE'S A MENACE AFTER ALL!

GNAH-HA!

All is peaceful in Beanotown...

SUDDENLY—

HORRIBLE DIN

EEK!

SQUAWK!

YIKES!

BAWL!

WOOF!

SCREECH!

AWFUL RACKET!

PESKY "DENNIS AND THE DINMAKERS" DISTURBING THE PEACE!

SHAKE

TREMBLE

BOOM-DA-BOOM!

OUR LULLABY CHOIR IS MUCH MORE SOOTHING.

SOFTIES

SO—

"GOLDEN SLUMBERS KISS YOUR EYES..."

HMM! THAT GIVES ME AN IDEA!

HOME HELP

MY MOUSE NEEDS A NEW HOME.

LOOK WHAT I'VE GOT!

SOFTY WALTER

A MUSICAL-BOX!

TARA-LA...

COME AND SEE MY MUSICAL-BOX, CHUMMIES.

MORE SOFT BOYS

SQUEAL! A MOUSE!

TARA-LA..

SWING IT, GIRL!

SWOON

LOOKS LIKE I'VE FOUND HIM A HOUSE!

'NIGHT, 'NIGHT!

Later—

MY ALLIGATOR'S OUTGROWN HIS TANK.

HM!

DENNIS FAN

I'LL FIND HIM A HOME.

Later— I'LL TEST THE WATER.

DENNIS'S DAD

YEOWP!

NIP!

I'M GOOD AT FINDING HOMES!

Soon—

BZZZ!

SHATTER!

GNAW!

AW! THE BIRD'S LOST ITS NEST!

So—

EEK!

WIG

I'VE FOUND YOU A NEW HOME!

I'M GREAT AT FINDING HOMES FOR PEOPLE.

REALLY?

SEE IF YOU CAN GET ANYONE FOR THESE HOMES, THEN! NO-ONE WILL BUY A HOUSE WITHIN TWO MILES OF A MENACE LIKE YOU!

FOR SALE

FOR SALE

FOR SALE